PowerKids Readers:

The Bilingual Library of the United States of America™

Bilingual Edition
English/Spanish
Edición bilingüe

WEST VIRGINIA

VIRGINIA OCCIDENTAL

JENNIFER WAY

TRADUCCIÓN AL ESPAÑOL: MARÍA CRISTINA BRUSCA

The Rosen Publishing Group's
PowerKids Press™ & **Editorial Buenas Letras**™
New York

Published in 2006 by The Rosen Publishing Group, Inc.
29 East 21st Street, New York, NY 10010

First Edition

Photo Credits: Cover, pp. 25, 30 (Capital) © Craig Cunningham/Getty Images; pp. 5, 30 (state motto) © Joe Sohm/The Image Works; pp. 5 (state seal), 26 © One Mile Up, Inc.; p. 7 © 2002 Geoatlas; pp. 9, 13, 17, 31 (Buck, Denver) © Bettmann/Corbis; p. 11 © Underwood & Underwood/Corbis; p. 15 Library of Congress Geography and Map Division; p. 19 © Steve Jessee/Associated Photo; pp. 21, 31 (hiking) © Paul Harris/Getty Images; p. 23 Courtesy Avampato Discovery Museum; p. 30 (rhododendron) © Michael T. Sedam/Corbis; p. 30 (cardinal) © Gary W. Carter/Corbis; p. 30 (mountain state) © David Muench/Corbis; p. 30 (sugar maple) © Robert Estall/Corbis; p. 31(Jackson) © The Corcoran Gallery of Art/Corbis; p. 31(Knotts) © A. S. Adler/IPOL/Globe Photos, Inc.; p. 31 (Retton) © Neal Preston/Corbis; p. 31 (Garner) © Graham Whitby-Boot/Allstar/Globe Photos, Inc.; p. 31 (bungee) © Mike Powell/Corbis; p. 31 (coal) © Claudius/zefa/Corbis.

Library of Congress Cataloging-in-Publication Data

Way, Jennifer.
    West Virginia / Jennifer Way ; traducción al español, María Cristina Brusca.— 1st ed.
        p. cm. — (The bilingual library of the United States of America)
    Includes bibliographical references and index.
    ISBN 1-4042-3114-5 (library binding)
    1. West Virginia—Juvenile literature. I. Title. II. Series.
F241.3.W39 2006
975.4—dc22
                                                                    2005032644

Manufactured in the United States of America

Due to the changing nature of Internet links, Editorial Buenas Letras has developed an online list of Web sites related to the subject of this book. This site is updated regularly. Please use this link to access the list:

http://www.buenasletraslinks.com/ls/westvirginia

Contents

Contenido

Welcome to West Virginia

West Virginia is the tenth-smallest state in the United States. West Virginia is known as the Mountain State. The Appalachian Mountains run through West Virginia.

Bienvenidos a Virginia Occidental

Por su tamaño, Virginia Occidental es el décimo estado más pequeño de los Estados Unidos. Es llamado el Estado Montañoso. Los montes Apalaches atraviesan Virginia Occidental.

West Virginia Flag and State Seal

Bandera y escudo de Virginia Occidental

West Virginia Geography

West Virginia is in the Southeast of the United States. West Virginia borders the states of Kentucky, Ohio, Maryland, Pennsylvania, and Virginia.

Geografía de Virginia Occidental

Virginia Occidental está en el sureste de los Estados Unidos. Virginia Occidental linda con los estados de Kentucky, Ohio, Maryland, Pensilvania y Virginia.

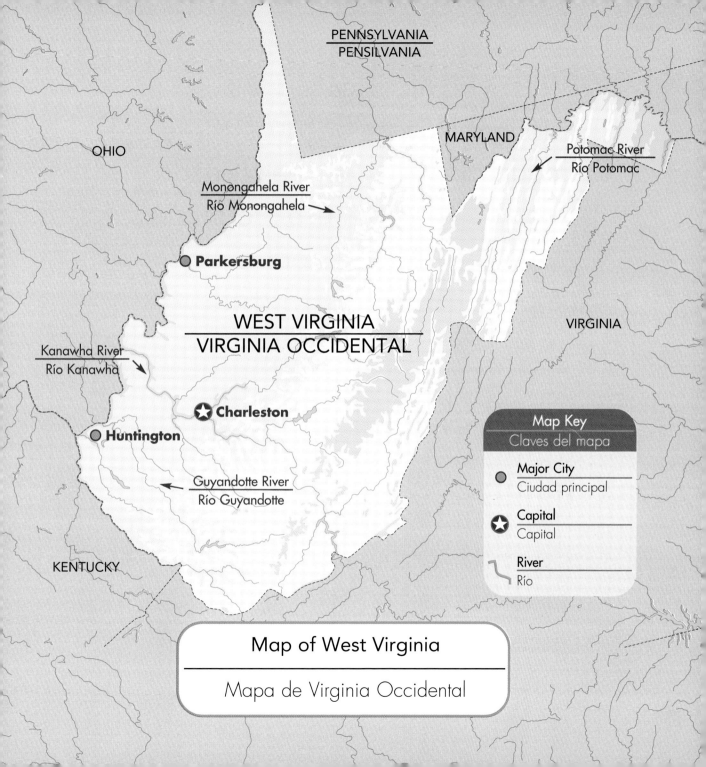

PENNSYLVANIA
PENSILVANIA

OHIO

MARYLAND

Potomac River
Río Potomac

Monongahela River
Río Monongahela

● **Parkersburg**

WEST VIRGINIA
VIRGINIA OCCIDENTAL

VIRGINIA

Kanawha River
Río Kanawha

★ **Charleston**

● **Huntington**

Guyandotte River
Río Guyandotte

Map Key
Claves del mapa

● Major City
Ciudad principal

★ Capital
Capital

River
Río

KENTUCKY

Map of West Virginia

Mapa de Virginia Occidental

West Virginia is called the Mountain State because there are mountains all over the state. Many places in these mountains have coal. Mining coal is important for West Virginia.

Virginia Occidental es llamado el Estado Montañoso porque hay montañas en todo el estado. Muchas de estas montañas tienen carbón. Las minas de carbón son importantes para Virginia Occidental.

ATT. MINERS.
WERE ON THE BITUMINOUS
...COAL FRONT...
Underground Movement AMERICAN STYLE
COAL MAKES · TNT · RUBBER · SULPHA DRUGS
AND 100 OTHER WAR PRODUCTS
THIS IS OUR FOX HOLE
DIG IN !!! UNDERMINE THE AXIS
POCAHONTAS OPERATORS ASS'N. BLUEFIELD, W.VA.

1943   NO. 34 MINE

West Virginia Coal Miners in 1944

Mineros del carbón en Virginia Occidental en 1944

West Virginia History

The Baltimore & Ohio Railroad came to West Virginia in 1837. Railroads connected the state to many cities. Coal from West Virginia powered trains. These things helped West Virginia grow.

Historia de Virginia Occidental

El ferrocarril Baltimore & Ohio llegó a Virginia Occidental en 1837. Los ferrocarriles conectaron al estado con muchas ciudades. El carbón de Virginia Occidental propulsaba los trenes. Todo esto contribuyó al crecimiento del estado.

The Atlantic Train on the Baltimore & Ohio Railroad

El tren Atlantic del ferrocarril Baltimore & Ohio

John Brown was born in 1800. He believed slavery was wrong. In 1859, he led a group of men to attack an army building in Harpers Ferry, West Virginia. He wanted to take the guns there and use them to set slaves free.

John Brown nació en 1800. Brown creía que la esclavitud era injusta. En 1859, condujo a un grupo de hombres en el ataque a un edificio del ejército, en Harpers Ferry, Virginia Occidental. Brown quería apoderarse de las armas para liberar a los esclavos.

John Brown

West Virginia was part of Virginia until 1861. That year the Civil War began, and Virginia broke away from the United States. The people of western Virginia did not agree with this. They broke away from Virginia and formed West Virginia.

Virginia Occidental fue parte de Virginia hasta 1861. Ese año comenzó la Guerra Civil y Virginia se separó de los Estados Unidos. La gente que vivía en el oeste de Virginia no estuvo de acuerdo, se separó de Virginia, y formó Virginia Occidental.

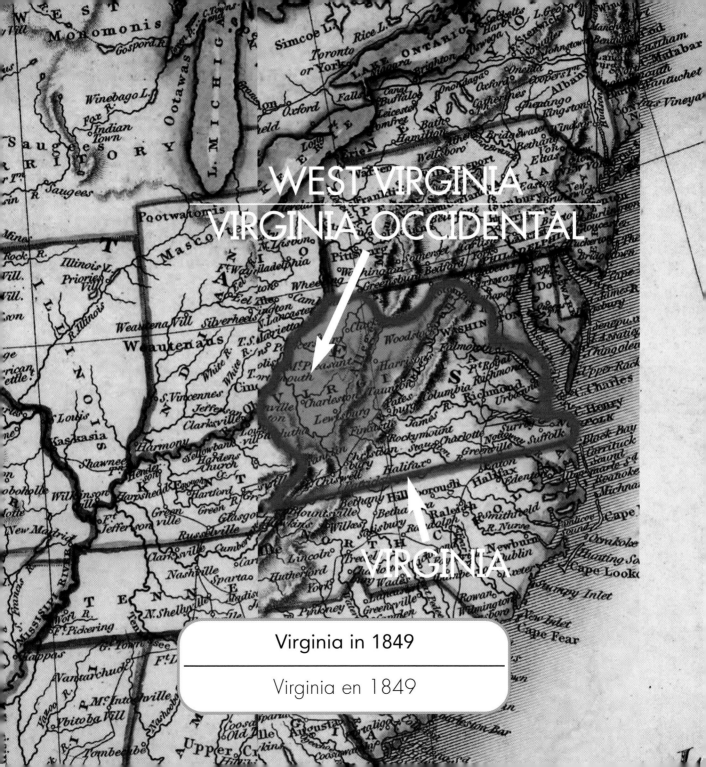

WEST VIRGINIA
VIRGINIA OCCIDENTAL

VIRGINIA

Virginia in 1849
_____
Virginia en 1849

Mary Harris Jones was born in Ireland in 1837. People called her "Mother Jones." Beginning in the 1890s, she helped coal miners in West Virginia fight for better working conditions.

Mary Harris Jones nació en Irlanda en 1837. La gente la llamó "Madre Jones". A comienzos de los años 1890, Jones ayudó a los mineros del carbón en su lucha para mejorar sus condiciones de trabajo.

Mother Jones (1830–1930)

Madre Jones (1830-1930)

Living in West Virginia

There are many fun festivals in West Virginia. On Bridge Day people celebrate the New River Gorge Bridge, which was finished in 1977. You can watch people bungee jump from the bridge on Bridge Day!

La vida en Virginia Occidental

En Virginia Occidental hay muchos festivales divertidos. En el Día del puente, la gente celebra el puente New River Gorge. ¡Ese día puedes ver cómo la gente practica salto *bungee* desde el puente!

Bungee Jumping on Bridge Day

Salto *bungee* en el Día del puente

People enjoy hiking in West Virginia's mountains. A famous place to hike is the Appalachian Trail. It runs through the Appalachian Mountains in West Virginia and in 13 other states. The trail is 2,174 miles (3,500 km) long!

Mucha gente disfruta de los paseos a pie por las montañas de Virginia Occidental. La ruta de los Apalaches es un lugar famoso para caminar. Esta ruta atraviesa los montes Apalaches de Virginia Occidental y cruza otros 13 estados. ¡Esta ruta mide 2,174 millas (3,500 km)!

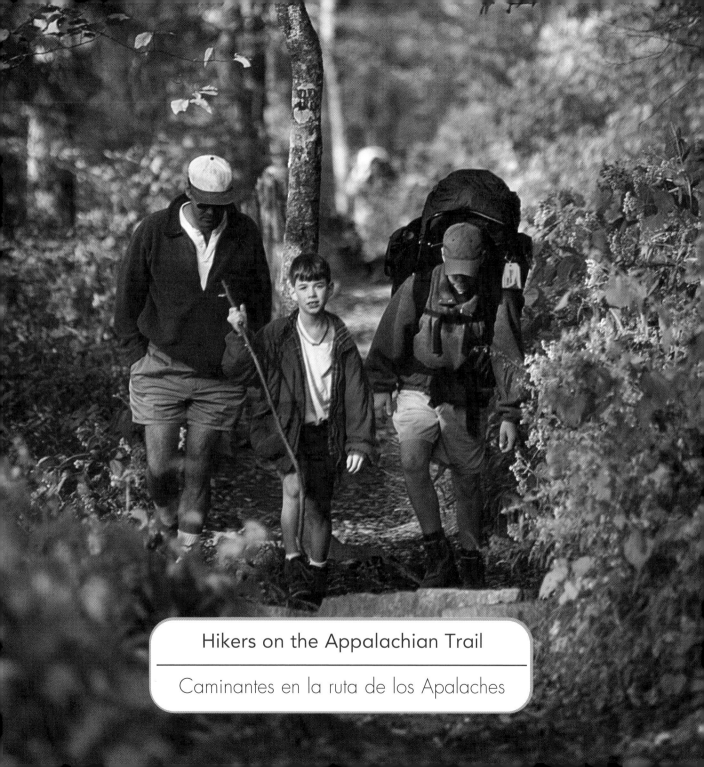

Hikers on the Appalachian Trail

Caminantes en la ruta de los Apalaches

West Virginia Today

The Avampato Discovery Museum in Charleston is a fun place to visit. In this museum children can learn how West Virginia's mountains were formed.

Virginia Occidental, hoy

Visitar el museo Avampato Discovery, en Charleston, es muy divertido. En este museo los niños pueden aprender cómo se formaron las montañas de Virginia Occidental.

The Avampato Discovery Museum

Museo Avampato Discovery

Charleston, Huntington, Parkersburg, and Wheeling are the biggest cities in West Virginia. Charleston is the capital of the state of West Virginia.

Charleston, Huntington, Parkersburg y Wheeling son las ciudades más grandes de Virginia Occidental. Charleston es la capital de Virginia Occidental.

Capitol Building in Charleston, West Virginia

Capitolio de Charleston en Virginia Occidental

Activity:
Let's Draw the West Virginia Seal

Actividad:
Dibujemos el escudo de Virginia Occidental

1

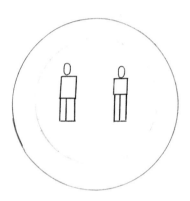

Make two circles, one inside the other. Draw the shapes of the men.

Traza dos círculos, uno adentro del otro. Dibuja las formas de los dos hombres.

2

Add the men's clothes and their faces. Draw the rock between the men. Write June 20, 1863, on the rock.

Agrega los trajes y las caras de los hombres. Dibuja una roca entre los hombres. Escribe en la roca la fecha: June 20, 1863.

3

Draw the men's tools, the barrels and the ground.

Dibuja las herramientas de los hombres, los barriles y el suelo.

4

Write STATE OF WEST VIRGINIA and MONTANI SEMPER LIBERI on the seal.

Escribe en el escudo: STATE OF WEST VIRGINIA y MONTANI SEMPER LIBERI.

5

Add shading and detail. Great job!

Agrega sombras y detalles. ¡Muy bien!

Timeline		Cronología
The Virginia Colony is settled by the English.	**1607**	Los ingleses establecen la colonia de Virginia.
The Baltimore & Ohio Railroad comes to West Virginia.	**1837**	El ferrocarril Baltimor & Ohio llega a Virginia Occidental.
John Brown leads an attack at Harpers Ferry.	**1859**	John Brown conduce el ataque a Harpers Ferry.
West Virginia breaks away from Virginia.	**1861**	Virginia Occidental se separa de Virginia.
West Virginia becomes the thirty-fifth state.	**1863**	Virginia Occidental se convierte en el estado treinta y uno.
Charleston becomes the state capital.	**1885**	Charleston pasa a ser la capital del estado.
Miners begin to strike for better working conditions. Striking lasts nearly 10 years.	**1912**	Los mineros comienzan una huelga para mejorar las condiciones de trabajo. La huelga se prolonga por casi 10 años.
The Reber Radio Telescope is built in Green Bank.	**1937**	Se construye el telescopio Reber Radio en Green Bank.
The New River Gorge Bridge is finished.	**1977**	Se termina la construcción del puente New River Gorge.

West Virginia Events/
Eventos en Virginia Occidental

March
West Virginia Maple Syrup
Festival in Pickins

April
International Ramp Festival in Elkins

May
Scottish Heritage Festival and Celtic
Gathering in Clarksburg
Vandalia Gathering in Charleston

October
Mountain State Forest
Festival in Elkins
Southern West Virginia Italian
Festival in Bluefield
Wirt County Pioneer Days
in Elizabeth
Helvetia Swiss Day in Helvetia
Buffalo Octoberfest in Buffalo

November
Pocahontas NRHS Train Show
in Bluefield
Winter Wonderland Extravaganza
in Lewisburg

December
Jack Frost Celebration, Whitegrass

Marzo
Festival del jarabe de arce *(maple)* de
Virginia Occidental, en Pickins

Abril
Festival internacional del puerro silvestre,
en Elkins

Mayo
Festival de las tradiciones escocesas y
reunión celta, en Clarksburg
Reunión Vandalia, en Charleston

Octubre
Festival de los bosques del Estado
Montañoso, en Elkins
Festival italiano del sur de Virginia
Occidental, en Bluefield
Días de los pioneros del condado de
Wirt, en Elizabeth
Días suizos de Helvetia, en Helvetia
Octoberfest de Buffalo, en Buffalo

Noviembre
Exposición de trenes Pocahontas NRHS,
en Bluefield
Fiesta invernal de las maravillas,
en Lewisburg

Diciembre
Celebraciones Jack Frost, en Whitegrass

29

West Virginia Facts/
Datos sobre Virginia Occidental

Population
1.8 million

Población
1.8 million

Capital
Charleston

Capital
Charleston

State Motto
Montani semper liberi,
Mountaineers are
always free

Lema del estado
Montani semper liberi
(Montañeses por
siempre libres)

State Flower
Rhododendron

Flor del estado
Rododendro

State Bird
Cardinal

Ave del estado
Cardenal

State Nickname
Mountain State

Mote del estado
Estado Montañoso

State Tree
Sugar Maple

Árbol del estado
Arce azucarero

State Song
"West Virginia
My Home"

Canción del estado
"Virginia Occidental
es mi hogar"

Famous West Virginians/
Virginianos famosos

Thomas Jackson
(1824–1863)

Confederate general
General confederado

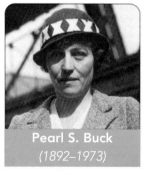

Pearl S. Buck
(1892–1973)

Writer
Escritora

Don Knotts
(1924–   )

Actor
Actor

Bob Denver
(1935–2005)

Actor
Actor

Mary Lou Retton
(1968–   )

Gymnast
Gimnasta

Jennifer Garner
(1972–   )

Actress
Actriz

Words to Know/Palabras que debes saber

border
frontera

bungee jump
salto *bungee*

coal
carbón

hiking
pasear a pie

31

Here are more books to read about West Virginia:
Otros libros que puedes leer sobre Virginia Occidental:

In English/En inglés:

M Is for Mountain State:
A West Virginia Alphabet
by Mary Ann McCabe Riehle
Sleeping Bear Press, 2004

West Virginia
by Wende Fazio
Children's Press, 2000

Words in English: 340

Palabras en español: 360

Index

Índice